THE
OVERWOOD

THE OVERWOOD

GABRIELLE PRENDERGAST

orca currents

ORCA BOOK PUBLISHERS

Published in Canada and the United States in 2022 by Orca Book Publishers.
orcabook.com

Library and Archives Canada Cataloguing in Publication
Title: The overwood / Gabrielle Prendergast.
Names: Prendergast, Gabrielle, author.
Series: Orca currents.
Description: Series statement: Orca currents
Identifiers: Canadiana (print) 2021016655x | Canadiana (ebook) 20210166568 |
ISBN 9781459831964 (softcover) | ISBN 9781459831971 (PDF) | ISBN 9781459831988 (EPUB)
Classification: LCC PS8631.R448 O94 2022 | DDC jc813/.6—dc23

Library of Congress Control Number: 2021934063

Summary: In this high-interest accessible novel for middle-grade readers, 14-year-old Blue Jasper
has to face an old foe from Faerieland who has made her way into his world.

Orca Book Publishers is committed to reducing the consumption of
nonrenewable resources in the production of our books. We make
every effort to use materials that support a sustainable future.

Orca Book Publishers gratefully acknowledges the support for its publishing
programs provided by the following agencies: the Government of Canada,
the Canada Council for the Arts and the Province of British Columbia
through the BC Arts Council and the Book Publishing Tax Credit.

Edited by Tanya Trafford
Design by Ella Collier
Cover photography by Getty Images/Lorenzo Valdovinos / EyeEm
Author photo by Erika Forest

Printed and bound in Canada.

25 24 23 22 • 1 2 3 4

Chapter One

The Christmas market is crowded. It's always stressful. My brother and sister, Indigo and Violet, are hard to manage. Even at the best and calmest times. But at the Christmas market it's nearly impossible. They get distracted by tinsel. They poke their fingers into the cotton-candy machine. They want to buy everything.

"Look, Blue!" Violet says. "They have butterfly wings. Can I get some?"

I stare at her. Indigo snuffles with laughter.

"Why would you want fake plastic butterfly wings?" I ask. I lower my voice. "You have *real* wings."

"Oh yeah," Violet says.

Violet and Indigo are ten years old. They're twins. They're Faeries. They have magical powers. That's where most of my problems come from.

Indigo starts to wander away. Rosa, my dog, barks. She's magical too. I haven't figured out yet how magical. She can't talk. So she can't tell me.

"Indigo!" I snap after him. "Stay with us."

I don't like to get angry with the twins. But the last time they wandered off, I nearly died. So I've learned to be careful.

"We're just looking for a present for Mom," I say firmly. "That's it. We can't afford anything else."

"Why can't we use Faerie money?" Violet asks, pouting.

Faerie money is just leaves or scraps of paper. Faeries can use magic to make it look like money. That's called *glamouring*.

All Faeries use glamour when they're around humans. They use it to make themselves look human. The twins use it to hide their wings. Mom is okay with that. But Faerie money is forbidden. Paying with Faerie money is like stealing. It turns back into leaves or scrap paper in about an hour.

Violet drifts toward a handmade-lollipop display. I yank her back by her hood. I have Rosa on a leash. I wish I could put the twins on a leash too.

Rosa sniffs a puddle. Indigo trips over her and falls on his face. Violet laughs. Little sparkly bubbles come out of her mouth. That's new. She covers her mouth and stares at me. Her eyes are wide.

"I didn't know I could do that!" she says.

I look around. I don't think anyone saw the bubbles. No one here knows that the twins are magical. No one knows about magic at all. And Oren, the twins' Faerie brother, wants it to stay that way.

Humans can't find out about Faerieland. They would only ruin it.

That's why the twins aren't allowed to do magic here in the Overwood. That's what Faeries call the human world. There's a whole other set of woods that makes up Faerieland. There's the Crosswood. You have to go through the Crosswood to get anywhere. Then there's Nearwood and Farwood. And the Wherewood. And my friend Salix's wood, Merwood.

It's complicated. Everything about Faerie life is. Especially when you're an ordinary human boy like me. And you have a Faerie brother and sister.

Violet's magic is growing and changing. She is the queen of Nearwood. The wood gives her power.

She doesn't know how to control it yet. Her older brother, Oren, is king of Farwood. He takes care of the twins during the week. They stay with me and Mom on weekends.

"Be careful!" I say to Violet. "Cover your mouth when you laugh."

I put my arms around both of them. We head toward the candle-seller.

Mom loves candles.

$\Rightarrow \star \Leftarrow$

We spend nearly an hour in the candle shop. Violet and Indigo have to smell every candle. Violet says the one called Ocean Mist should smell like fish.

"Why would anyone want a candle that smelled like fish?" I ask.

"A cat might," Violet says.

Rosa barks as though she agrees.

Indigo likes the candles that smell like food.

"Can we get donuts?" he asks.

I glare at him. Mom feeds us organic food. But the twins eat everything else when they're in Faerieland. I mean *everything* else. Cakes. Pies. Roast rabbit and deer. Pigeon soup. Tiny blue eggs scrambled with dandelion stems.

Faerie food is very bad for humans. Last week I ate a magical candy Indigo gave me. I saw sparkles for hours. Indigo got a time-out.

Whenever we're in town, the twins want to eat junk. I'm not supposed to let them. But I still have to get them home in one piece. I think I need to bribe them.

"What about a lollipop?" I ask. I know the lollipops here are all natural and organic. "If you behave, we can get one each."

"Yay!" they both shout. Violet shoots one tiny flame out of her left thumb. Indigo snuffs it out with his mitten.

"Nice save," I say. His mitten is only a little bit singed. I'm calling that a win.

We leave the market. At last. The twins are quiet. That's one good thing about the lollipops. Just as we walk through the market entrance, I see something. Something out of place. I turn quickly. A woman is staring at us.

This is a small town. I know almost everyone. But I don't recognize her. She has long brown hair in braids. She's dressed all in black, old-fashioned clothes. I tug the twins through the gate quickly.

"Violet," I say, leaning down to whisper. "Do you see that woman by the cheese stall? The one all in black? Is she Fae?"

Violet can see through Faerie glamours. She glances back.

"No," she whispers after a second. "She's a human."

I turn just in time to see the woman duck around a corner. Maybe I panicked for nothing. But I'm always on edge now. The first time I went to Faerieland, Violet and I defeated the evil queen Olea. Violet took her place as Queen of Nearwood.

So Olea hates us. And she's already tried to kill me. More than once.

We hurry down to the bus stop. We don't have any snow. It rarely snows here. But it's cold. Indigo actually zips up his coat. He almost never does that.

We don't have to wait long for the bus. It will take us out of town and drop us at the top of our driveway. Driveway? It's more like a road. It's a ten-minute walk from the highway to our cottage.

We live in the middle of the forest. Mom calls it "off-grid." I guess I'm used to it. But that doesn't mean I like it. I'm older now. And I'm in high school. I need the internet. Or TV even. Or a phone. But Mom won't let me have any of that stuff. She likes us to live like cavemen. And all the trouble we've had with Faeries lately has just made it worse.

As the bus arrives I see something out of the corner of my eye. It's the woman from the market! She stands on the corner, staring. I shove Violet and Indigo onto the bus. Then I pick up Rosa and carry her on.

As the bus pulls away, the strange woman is still on the corner. Watching us.

Chapter Two

I feel uneasy when the bus turns onto the highway. The twins are sitting quietly. Rosa curls up at their feet. I sit across from them. By habit I check that we still have everything. The twins still have their coats. That's a miracle. I have the shopping bag with Mom's candle. I have my wallet. As I tuck my bus pass away, I feel something in my pocket. It's a marble.

I pull it out with a sigh. It's a simple glass marble with a wisp of gold inside. Indigo must have put it in there. Not long ago he and I got lost in the Wherewood. We met a witch there. She helped us. She also gave me this marble. I never knew why.

Indigo thinks the marble is magic. But lately I'm trying to keep magic out of my life. So I'd put the marble in my sock drawer. Indigo must have taken it out and put it in my pocket. He does that. I should be thankful it's not a spider or a worm. He's done that too.

It's just a possibly magic marble. It seems a small thing, but…

Once Faeries touch your life, nothing is the same. I love the twins. And I like my Faerie friends Salix and Finola. I even like King Oren. But everything else about Faerieland is dangerous and scary.

I've tried to talk to Mom. I think she understands. But it's hard for her to talk about it. Olea saved my life when I was a baby. So mom owed her a favor.

Owing a favor to a Faerie is really bad.

Olea made Mom pay back that favor by taking care of Indigo and Violet. Mom pretty much adopted them. That wasn't so bad. At first. But when Olea's rival took the twins away, it got bad fast. Olea threatened to kill me. Then she threatened to kill Mom. I barely managed to save everyone. I got a lot of help from Salix and Finola. Violet took Olea's place as Queen of Nearwood. She banished Olea to Witherwood. Witherwood is like a prison for bad Faeries.

But banishing Olea wasn't the end of it. Olea somehow tricked us all into going to Witherwood. We had a battle that very nearly cost us all our lives. But by then Violet had become very powerful. She took Olea's power and cast her out of Faerieland forever. She ended up here, in the human world.

So now I can't feel safe here either.

I tuck the marble back in my pocket. I make a mental note to hide it somewhere Indigo can't find it. I could throw it away. But then someone else might find it. And who knows what would happen then?

That's life when you have Faeries in your family. Nothing is certain. You never know what to expect. And you never feel safe.

The bus slows down and stops at the top of our road. I herd the twins and Rosa down the stairs. We all shout our thanks to the bus driver.

"Merry Christmas!" he shouts back.

"I'm hungry," Indigo says. His lollipop is long gone. It's lunchtime anyway. We got up early to go to the market first thing, before all the good stuff got sold.

"The faster you walk, the faster we'll be home," I say. "Mom will have lunch ready."

Indigo whoops and starts running down the road. I grab Violet's hand and run after him, pulling Rosa on her leash behind me.

$$\rightarrow \star \leftarrow$$

Just before we reach the bend in our road, Rosa starts to bark. She tugs hard on her leash. It slips from my fingers.

"Rosa! Stop!" I shout after her as she bolts away. I'm careful not to use her full name, Mrs. Rosa Guzman. If you know a Faerie's full name, you can command them three times. For three wishes. Rosa's not really a Faerie. She's a regular dog. But she absorbed some Faerie magic in the battle with Olea. And I did accidentally command her once. I don't know if I can do it again. Or if I can do it more than three times. She's a dog, after all. The Faerie rules might not apply quite the same. Anyway, you never know.

I might need another wish one day. I don't want to waste it.

We run after Rosa. Around the bend in our road, we can see the cottage. Rosa slides to a stop. She growls. She never growls.

"Rosa?" I say, catching up to her. "What's the matter?"

She growls again and crouches down. She slowly edges toward the house.

"What's going on?" Violet asks. "Why is she acting like that?"

"I don't know," I say. I grab Rosa's leash and pull her to a stop. Turning, I scan the trees around us. It's still just after midday, so the day is bright. But the trees are dense and dark. Anything could be hiding in there. Especially magical things.

I grab Violet by the shoulder and pull her toward me. I do the same with Indigo.

"Take your coats off," I say. "In case you need to fly."

Mom made special shirts for them. They have open flaps in the back so the twins' wings can come out.

"I'm not leaving you here," Violet says with a frown. "Not if there's some kind of danger."

"Me neither," Indigo says.

"Do what I tell you!" I snap. "I'll be fine. Rosa can protect me."

Rosa growls again, her nose pointed at the house.

Both twins slip off their coats and hold them. We edge a few steps closer.

"The front door is open," Violet says.

She's right. Mom likes fresh air. But it's December. It's cold. I don't think she would leave the door open today. For one thing, it would suck out all the heat from our woodstove.

When we're at the bottom of the stairs, I call out, "Mom?"

There's no answer. I turn to the twins.

"Wait here. If anything happens, *anything*, fly away. Understand?"

They glare at me. But I think they'll do what I say.

I pull Rosa close to me and tiptoe up the front stairs. Everything looks normal on the porch. The wooden chairs are where they usually are. When I reach the front door, I call out again.

"Mom?"

Still no answer. Our cottage is not very big. If Mom were inside, she would have heard me. I poke my head through the door.

My stomach drops.

Everything is turned over. Chairs toppled. Bookcase knocked down. A picture pulled off the wall and smashed. Lunch is half on the table and half on the floor. I run inside and check all the rooms.

"Mom! Mom?" I yell.

But she's gone.

Chapter Three

I make sure no one is in the house. Then I let the twins in.

"Mom's not here?" Violet says. Her eyes are wide again.

Indigo sniffs the air. "It smells like…"

"Strawberry jam?" I ask. Faerie magic often smells sweet. The first time I met Olea, I smelled strawberry jam. But how could Olea have been here?

"Violet," I ask, "you're sure Olea's magic is all gone? You took it all?"

"I'm sure," she says. "I asked Oren about it. He said that's how it works."

"It must have been other Faeries," I say. "Faeries that are loyal to Olea."

Indigo looks in the bedrooms, the bathroom and out in the yard.

"Maybe there is some other explanation," he says.

"An explanation for why Mom trashed the house and ran out? And left the door open?" I ask. "Like what?"

Indigo shrugs. "A swarm of bees?"

"It's winter, Indigo," Violet says. "The bees are hibernating."

Indigo looks thoughtful for a moment. And a little sad.

"Maybe Mom finally got fed up with us," he says in a small voice.

"What?" I say.

Violet takes his hand. She looks sad too.

"Maybe now that her pact with Olea is done," Violet says, "she doesn't need to take care of us anymore."

"No, don't say that." I kneel down so I can look directly into their faces. "Mom would never leave you. She loves you. *I* love you. We're a family."

Violet and Indigo look at each other.

"We're difficult," Violet says.

"We put you and Mom in danger all the time," Indigo says.

He's not wrong. But that doesn't mean Mom would leave them. Or that I would leave them. I would never leave them.

I stand up and go over to one of the kitchen drawers. Opening it, I find Mom's wallet. And her keys.

"Look," I say. "She left everything behind. And if she was going to leave you, why would she wreck the house?"

The twins shrug. They still look sad. I gather them into a hug. Leaning back, I look into their faces. Faeries are unnaturally beautiful. The twins are no exception. Their faces are perfect. They have smooth skin and large, bright blue eyes. Their hair is thick and shiny. They could be in a magazine. Next to them I look like a troll. It used to bother me, but now…

Well, now I know what they are, so it makes sense. For a little while I was jealous. I wanted to be magical too. But when we fought Olea in Witherwood, I learned that magic is way too scary for me. Oren once told me it can be both a curse and a blessing. I didn't believe him at the time, but I know now what he means.

Violet and Indigo look up at me with their sad eyes.

"Anyway," I say. "If Mom left us, it might be because of me. I'm failing math *and* gym."

That makes them smile.

"Let's go search the forest," I suggest.

⇛ ★ ⇚

The forest behind our cottage is where all this Faerie stuff started. There's a spot about ten minutes in where the boundary between the human and Faerie worlds becomes thin. There are places like that all over. And you can get through them into the Crosswood.

We go there first. If Mom has been taken back to Faerieland, this is the way it was done. We run the whole way there and arrive panting. The forest looks like it always does. Even though it's winter, there's still a lot of green. It never gets very cold here. Some trees lose their leaves in the fall, but some don't. And there are pine trees and moss that stay green all year round.

A spiky, twisted tree marks the entrance to the Crosswood. It looks just the same too. I don't see any tracks on the path except for ours.

"Should we go to the Crosswood to look for her?" Indigo asks.

I frown at the spiky tree. If someone wanted to trap the twins, this would be a perfect way to do it. Lure them into the Crosswood by taking Mom. The Crosswood is not as well guarded as the royal courts in Nearwood and Farwood. And Oren thinks there are Faeries, and other creatures, that are still loyal to Olea.

Faerieland is just as messed up as the human world in some ways.

"No, definitely not," I say. "It could be a trap."

Violet suddenly gasps. She ducks around the other side of the spiky tree. I dash after her. Indigo and Rosa follow.

We find Violet staring intently at something that looks like a firefly. It's not, of course. It's a

Will-o'-the-Wisp, a kind of tiny Faerie. Violet says a few words to it in a language I don't understand. Indigo says a few more words in the same language. This is the Will-o'-the-Wisp language. The twins have been speaking it since they were little. I used to think it was just one of those made-up languages twins sometimes have. But it's not.

Violet finally turns to me as the Will-o'-the-Wisp drifts off.

"It's going to take a message to Oren," she says. "It doesn't think Mom is in Faerieland."

"Where is she then?" Indigo asks. He's starting to sound frantic. Indigo never sounds frantic.

"I don't know," Violet says. "Hopefully Oren will have some idea."

I glance up at the spiky tree again. I wish I'd never seen it. I wish this portal to the Crosswood didn't exist. We'd all be a lot happier. And safer. But then I guess I never would have met Violet and Indigo. I wouldn't be their brother.

I sigh and tug them both back onto the main path to the cottage.

"Let's wait for Oren at home," I say. "He'll know to look for us there. And you two still need to eat lunch. So does Rosa."

Chapter Four

While we wait to hear back from Oren, I make the twins some lunch. All I can manage is toast and cheese slices, but they devour it. I have a piece of toast too, even though I'm not hungry. Rosa eats a bowl of dog kibble. While the twins clean up, I gather a few things.

I have a feeling I'm about to go on another adventure. I want to be prepared this time.

Properly prepared. I tie an extra sweater around my waist. I tuck some dog treats in my coat pockets. I take the money out of Mom's wallet. I know she was probably saving it for Christmas presents. But if Mom's in the human world, I might need money to find her.

She could be anywhere. Australia. The North Pole. Timbuktu or Tokyo. Somehow that's even more scary than her being in Faerieland. Apart from Faerieland I've never been very far from home.

An hour after we sent the message, Oren appears in our backyard. He's wearing a long red cloak and a holly crown. He looks like a very young Santa Claus.

"Sorry I took so long," he says, coming up the back stairs. "I had to consult my seers."

I'd love to know what seers are, but we don't have time. I usher him inside.

The twins are sitting quietly on the couch. Oren is their big brother, and a king, so they always try to behave around him. Unlike with me. They only try to behave about half the time with me.

I sit between them. Rosa lies down at my feet. Oren perches on the edge of Mom's favorite chair.

"I'm afraid that Olea did take your mother," Oren says.

Violet and Indigo look at me. I put my arms around them as Oren continues.

"My seers told me that Olea has managed to hire a human witch. This witch has gathered a lot of wild magic in the Faerie Woods. She is almost as powerful as a Faerie."

"Where have they taken Mom?" I ask. "And why? Why did they take her?"

Oren looks grave. He takes a breath and speaks slowly.

"Just before I left my palace, I received a message. From Olea."

"What did it say?" Violet asks.

"Olea has taken your mother to a place called Toronto," Oren says. "Do you know where that is?"

"Toronto?" I say. "*The* Toronto? That's on the other side of the country. It's thousands of miles from here!"

Oren frowns at me. "Don't worry about that," he says. "There are ways to travel there quickly. But…"

"What?" I ask.

Oren looks down at his hands. He has gold rings on every finger, and his fingernails are painted green. When he looks back up at me, his eyes are sad. Scared even. Oren doesn't scare easily.

"Olea's message was very clear," he says. "She wants you, Blue, to come to collect your mother before the sunrise on the solstice. Or she dies."

"The solstice!" Violet cries. "December 21? But that's tomorrow!"

Oren slides out of the chair and kneels in front of us. He puts one hand on my knee, the other on Rosa's head.

"You must understand, Blue," he says. "I think Olea means to lure you there to kill you."

I try to stay calm, but it's hard. My mouth is dry. I clutch a tuft of Rosa's fur at her neck. She whines and leans back on me.

"Why does Olea want to kill me?" I croak out. "Revenge?"

Oren sits on his heels. "I don't know," he says. "It may be more than that. She may be trying to get her magic back." He pauses and looks at me sadly again. "I don't know much about human witchcraft. But I do know there are powerful spells that involve...firstborn sons."

31

My stomach lurches. "*I'm* a firstborn son."

"I know," Oren says. "The most powerful time for witches to do magic is on the winter solstice. Especially this year, as it's a full moon too. It might be best if I hide you all in Farwood Castle until it's over."

I look at the twins on either side of me. They are staring up at me with their large blue eyes.

"But won't that mean..." I swallow, struggling to go on. "Won't that mean that Olea will kill Mom? I'm not going to just let her die!"

Oren shakes his head. He stands and paces across the floor. "If I didn't help you get to your mother, what would you do?"

I only need to think for a second. "I'd probably rob a bank or a store. And then steal a car. Drive to the airport. Get a plane ticket. Or hijack a plane."

Oren looks like he's trying not to laugh. Faeries are always a little amused by humans. Even when things are very serious.

"Well, I don't want you to do that," he says.

"Fine. I will take the twins to Farwood Castle—"

The twins start to object. Oren silences them with a stern look.

"I'll keep them safe there," Oren continues. "I will send you, Blue, through the Crosswood to Toronto. Rosa can go with you. But once you're there, you'll have to find your mother yourself. I don't have any other information."

"But how will he—?" Violet starts. This time I shush her.

"Never mind that," I say. "There's no time to waste. Is there?"

"No," Oren agrees. "Gather your things. Quickly."

I'm ready in under a minute. I have a backpack with extra clothes, food and some other supplies. And I have money. Oren leads us all back into the forest. We reach the spiky tree. He slips us magically through to the Crosswood. After another short walk we find an unusual sculpture. It's shaped like a woman lying down. But it's all blobby. There's a hole where her stomach should be.

Oren holds his hands out to me. "Take this," he says.

I can't see anything. But I know what it is. The first time I went to Faerieland, my friend Finola magically made me a sword. An invisible sword. I gave it to Oren. I don't have much need for a sword in my ordinary life. At least, I thought I didn't. Now he's giving it back.

I reach forward. My hand clasps the cold metal hilt. Just as Oren lets go, the sword shimmers into view. Now only I can see it. That's how "ghost swords" work.

Oren touches my shoulder. He squeezes it.

"Be careful, Blue Jasper," he says. "The place to start looking is among the human witches. If you can find them, I think you can find your mother."

"Okay," I say. I'm trying to act brave. But I'm already trembling.

"I'm going to send you some help," Oren says. "They will meet you in Toronto. Now. You must leave at once. Go through the statue."

He points at the blobby woman's stomach. I take a last look at Violet and Indigo. I pick Rosa up. Then we climb onto the statue and wriggle through the hole where the stomach should be.

I get a weird feeling. Like I'm being sucked into a vacuum cleaner. Rosa gives one high-pitched bark. Then everything goes black.

Chapter Five

I land with a *bonk*.

"Sir, please don't climb on the sculpture," a voice says.

When I blink I see someone standing over me. Someone in a uniform.

"Pardon me?" I ask.

The person, an older woman, points behind me. "The sculpture. It's not a toy."

I turn and look. The same sculpture that was in the Crosswood is behind me. But I'm not in the Crosswood anymore. I'm in some kind of gallery. There are other sculptures around me. They all look weird and blobby.

"I'm sorry," I say to the woman.

"Also, dogs are not allowed," she says. "Unless it's a registered support animal. You'll have to leave." She frowns at me before striding away. The back of her shirt says *volunteer guide*. Where am I?

"This place is creepy," another voice says. A familiar voice this time. My Faerie friends, Salix and Finola, appear from behind a sculpture. "Are these people who have been turned to stone?" Salix asks.

Finola rolls her eyes.

"They're sculptures," I say. "We don't turn people to stone in the human world." *No, we do much worse things.* But I keep that to myself.

Salix and Finola look different. They're wearing human clothes. And Salix's skin and hair, which are normally green, are brownish. Finola's feather crown, which I think is part of her hair, is hidden by a white knitted hat. They don't look like Faeries anymore. They look human.

I lead them over to a wide doorway. It's the entrance to this gallery. A sign says *Art Gallery of Ontario*. That's in Toronto. The sign says some other stuff about the sculptures, but I ignore that. At least I know I'm in the right city.

"Oren sent you?" I ask Salix and Finola as we leave the weird sculptures.

"Yeah," Salix says. "We're looking for a witch?"

"And your mother?" Finola adds.

"Yes," I say. "Olea has her. She plans to kill her. Or me. Or both of us."

"So...business as usual," Salix says.

"Apparently," I say. "This is my life now."

As we approach the exit of the building, I see a shadow out of the corner of my eye. I turn quickly. Down the end of a long passageway someone moves. They duck into the women's bathroom.

"What's the matter?" Finola asks.

I stare down the passage, but the woman doesn't come out. "Maybe nothing," I say. "I thought I saw a woman. I saw her earlier today too. In my town." I look down at Rosa. Her fur is standing on end. She is definitely unnerved. So am I.

"Maybe it's a coincidence," Salix says. "Just because the same woman is here doesn't mean she followed you."

"You don't understand," I tell him. "My town is thousands of miles away. It takes, like, six hours to get here, even by plane. I saw her"—I look at my watch—"about two hours ago. So there's no way she could get here. Unless…"

"Unless she used magic," Finola says.

Rosa growls and presses against my leg protectively. I don't think she likes the word *magic*. Neither do I, if I'm honest.

"Oren told us we are looking for a witch," Salix says. "What if that's her? Maybe we should go talk to her."

Just then two museum guards call out to us. "Hey! You kids can't bring a dog in here!"

"We're leaving!" I shout. Salix might be right about the woman. But I have a bad feeling. And I want to figure out exactly where we are first. I lead Rosa through the main entrance and onto the street. Salix and Finola follow.

⇒ ★ ⇐

It's dark outside. At first I'm confused. It should be about three o'clock. But then I remember I'm halfway across the country. In another time zone. It's probably six or seven o'clock here.

And it's *freezing*. I've never been so cold in my life. I zip up my coat and pull a scarf and mittens out of my backpack. I also pull out Rosa's raincoat. I slip it on her and then bundle myself up too.

"Are you two cold?" I ask Salix and Finola as we start walking.

"We're fine," Finola says. "We're wearing Faerie cloaks."

"You are?" I look at them. They're lit up by colorful streetlights. But their clothes look normal. And not warm enough for this weather. Salix is wearing a denim jacket over a green hoodie. Finola is wearing a fuzzy short coat over a minidress and black tights.

"The cloaks are glamoured," Salix explains. "So are we."

"I was wondering why you look so…different. So human," I say.

"Now that we're growing up, we're a lot better at using glamour," Salix says. "And other cool stuff."

"Yep," Finola says. "I have wings now. Like a swan. Wanna see?"

I take a small step away from her without meaning to. "No thanks," I say. I kind of do want to see the wings. But a busy street in Toronto is not the place.

"Do you have wings too?" I ask Salix.

"Unfortunately no," Salix says. "I can't fly. But I can turn into water. Very handy in Merwood."

I'd love to ask him to explain, but we don't have time. I need some information to help me find Mom.

Just around the corner I find exactly what I'm looking for. A library.

"I need to go in here," I say.

Salix peers through the glass doors. "What a large book collection! Is this a king's or a queen's palace? I hope they have a feast laid out."

"No…it's…" I try not to laugh. "This is a public library. It's a place to borrow books. But they have computers too and WiFi. I can get online and google some things. Figure out what to do next."

Salix and Finola look confused.

"None of those words made any sense," Finola says. "But okay."

We hurry inside. It's nice and warm. I'm not sure if they allow dogs. So we try to avoid the librarians. Luckily it's not very crowded. We get a computer straight away. I hide Rosa under the desk. I open a search page and type in *Toronto witches*.

One of the first hits is a store. It's called The Broom Closet. The map tells me it's only a few blocks away.

"This could work," I say. "Look."

Salix and Finola lean over my shoulders. We look at the store's website together. It sells spell books and tarot cards and things it claims are "magic potions." It's probably all fake. But it's a start. I click the link to customer photos. The page fills up with tiny thumbnail pictures.

Behind me, Finola gasps.

"What is it?" I ask.

She points to a tiny picture. I look closer.

"Oh…" I say. I click on the thumbnail and open the picture to full size.

It's definitely the woman I saw at the market this morning. The same woman I saw at the art gallery.

"That's her!" I say. "The one I saw earlier today."

"Why did you gasp, Finola?" Salix asks.

"I recognize her too," Finola says. "She's *definitely* a real witch. She's the one who turned me into a swan."

"The bog witch?" I ask. "Are you sure?"

When I first met Finola, she was in the form of

a swan because a bog witch cursed her. I helped her break the curse.

"I'm sure," Finola says. "She's a human witch too. Which is worse, given the circumstances."

Salix and I exchange a look.

"I'm not sure what you mean," I say.

Finola lowers her voice. "If she's working with Olea," she says gravely, "that means Olea is probably going to try the kind of magic you need a human for it to work."

"Like commanding using a full name?" That's the way Olea was defeated.

"Yes," Finola says. "Or something worse. She has your mother. She's a human. And Olea is basically a human now too. So if she's working with a witch, she has some other spell in mind."

The skin on the back of my neck prickles.

"What spell?" Salix asks.

"I don't know," Finola says.

I grab a piece of paper and pencil from the desk and write down the address of the store.

"We need to find this bog witch," I say. "Let's go to the store."

Chapter Six

The Broom Closet is only a five-minute walk from the library. But it's so cold that we all run the whole way. Just before we get there, it starts to snow.

"Pixies!" Salix yells up at the snowflakes. Several people turn to stare at us. Toronto streets are crowded. People are doing their Christmas shopping. Several of them carry two or three bags in each hand. It makes me feel bad about the small scented candle. That was all we could afford to buy for Mom.

I think I'll ask the twins to bring her something special from Faerieland. If I get out of this alive.

We find the store next to a dark alley. It doesn't seem to fit with the other stores. They're all colorful and well lit. The Broom Closet is dingy and ancient-looking. Peering through the dirty windows, I see it's cluttered and cramped inside. There's a sign on the door. It reads *Animal Familiars Welcome. Please Leash Them.*

I'm not sure what an "animal familiar" is. But Rosa is on a leash, so I open the door and head inside. Salix and Finola follow me.

Inside the store, a tiny bell goes *ting* as we enter. Seconds later a very tall, thin man appears from a back room. He's wearing ripped jeans, a bowler hat and a concert T-shirt of a band I like.

"Good evening," he says. "Can I help you find anything?"

I've never liked dealing with people in stores. I always get tongue-tied. But my mother's life is at stake. So I step forward and try to speak confidently.

"I have a question about your website," I say.

The bowler-hat man looks surprised. I notice his name tag reads *Kevin*. Doesn't seem like a very magical name. He steps behind a little counter. There's a computer on the counter. He swivels the screen toward me.

"Of course," he says. "Which product?"

I grab the computer mouse and click a couple of links.

"Not a product," I say. "A customer." I bring the picture of the bog witch up. "We're trying to find this woman. She…uh…has something of mine."

The way Kevin reacts tells me I'm in the right

place. He presses his lips together. He frowns and glares down at me.

"Customer information is private," he says.

"It's important," I say. "Someone's life is in danger."

"Look, kid," Kevin says. "We sell plastic junk and call it magical. No one is in danger from anything that goes on here."

I look around the store. Most of the products do look like plastic junk. Maybe we *are* in the wrong place. Surely if real witches shopped here there would be some things that looked like real magic.

"Either buy something or leave," Kevin says.

I turn to Finola and Salix. Salix is holding Rosa's leash. He's looking at some fake spiderwebs. But Finola is glaring at Kevin. Her dark eyes are intent.

"He's not Fae," she whispers so low I barely hear her.

"So?" I ask.

"So this," she says. She shrugs off her fluffy coat. Her glamour seems to shrug off at the same time. I turn back to Kevin. He's staring at her, horrified. Finola's feather crown reappears. Her swan wings shimmer into view behind her. She spreads them and waves them, making the T-shirts hanging on the wall flutter.

"Oh…my…goddess," Kevin says. He edges toward the door to the back room. "Come right this way."

Finola smirks at me. "Humans," she says. "So easy to intimidate."

$$\Rightarrow \star \Leftarrow$$

The back room looks very different from the front of the store. Everything in the front looked fake and plastic. Everything back here looks ancient and mysterious. And the back room is surprisingly large. Kevin leads us down to a table at the far end. We pass shelves and shelves of books and bottles. Silver goblets line one shelf. Gold mugs line another. There are gleaming swords and daggers in a rack. A cabinet shelf sags under the weight of hundreds of jars filled with marbles.

Marbles! I think of the one in my pocket. The one the witch gave me in the Wherewood. Slowing down, I see one jar full of what seems to be the same kind. Clear glass with a wisp of gold inside. The jar has a smudged label. It might say *friend finder*. But it could be *fiend finder*. Seems like an important distinction.

"What are these?" I ask.

Kevin turns. "Ah, blessing spheres," he says. "Witches often like to give those to people who are doing business with them. A gift-with-purchase kind of thing. They are simple spells anyone can use. Even non-witches."

"How do they work?" I ask.

Kevin adjusts his bowler hat, looking important. "Well, first a witch has to activate them, so don't get any ideas. You can't just grab a handful," Kevin says, looking me up and down. I know my clothes are a bit shabby. Mom gets everything secondhand. But that's no reason to think I'm a criminal.

"I wasn't going to," I say. "I'm not a thief."

"Hmm," Kevin says. "Anyway, if the blessing sphere *is* activated, you simply crush it under your foot and that releases the spell."

"What does—" I start, but Finola interrupts me.

"Blue," she says sharply. "We don't have time."

Kevin sits at a chair at the table. We all sit across from him. I put my hand on the hilt of my ghost sword. It makes me feel a bit more secure.

"What do you want with Barbara?" Kevin asks.

"Who?" I say, confused.

"Barbara," Kevin repeats. "The witch in the picture on our website?"

"Her name is *Barbara*?" Salix says with a snicker. "Barbara the Bog Witch?"

Finola shushes him.

"I think she's involved in kidnapping my mother," I say. I explain the rest of what I know. Kevin listens intently. He doesn't seem at all surprised to hear about Faeries and magic and magical woods.

"There are no Faerie witches in Toronto," Kevin says. "Barbara is a human witch. Human witches can only do limited kinds of magic in the human world."

"Overwood," I murmur.

He nods. "That's right. In the Faerie Woods witches are able to use wild magic. Do you know what that is?"

"Unfortunately, yes," I say. Wild magic can be useful. But it is also very dangerous. I learned that the last time I faced Olea.

"Well, Barbara wouldn't have magic powerful enough to get your mother from the other side of the country. So she must have Faeries working with her."

"Faeries loyal to Olea," Salix says in a low voice.

"Olea of Nearwood?" Kevin says, his eyebrows rising. "You got on *her* bad side? You're brave."

"I didn't have much choice," I say tightly. "Olea has my mother somewhere in Toronto. And she plans to kill her. Or me. Or both of us."

Kevin scratches his head. "Most of the human witches here are fairly harmless. But Barbara...she can be a lot sometimes."

"Yes," Finola says. "We've had run-ins with her before."

"Where can I find her?" I ask.

Kevin looks as though he doesn't want to tell me. But then he sighs.

"I haven't seen Barbara in a while. But one of the other witches might know where she is," he says. "The local witches meet at St. James Cemetery. And there's a meeting tonight. At midnight."

And I thought this day couldn't get worse.

Chapter Seven

It's even colder outside when we leave the store. I end up carrying Rosa inside my coat. This keeps us both warmer. It's still snowing. I've always thought snow is pretty. But it never gets this cold where I live. Even when it snows, which is rarely.

Following a rough map Kevin drew for us, we tromp through the dark Toronto streets. I try to think of what to do once we find the witches.

We get to the graveyard well before midnight. So I have some time to think. We sit on the crumbling church stairs. I'm glad I took the extra minute before I left to pack some provisions. I give Rosa dog kibble and some apple slices. I eat two muffins and a boiled egg. I offer a muffin to Salix. He sniffs it suspiciously.

"My mom made them," I say.

"What's in them?" he asks.

"Oats, rice bran and shredded carrot," I say.

Salix makes a face and sets the muffin back into the bag delicately. "No, thank you," he says.

I feel my cheeks get hot. I've been made fun of at school for the food Mom makes me. Other kids have ham sandwiches on white bread. Or they get money to buy lunch. I get yam-and-sunflower-seed salad. It's good actually. I like it. And I know it's healthy. But I don't enjoy being teased.

Finola mutters something, and two steaming cups appear, one in each of her hands.

"Ooh, spiced wine," Salix says, grabbing one.

I'm about to tell them kids aren't allowed to drink alcohol. But then I remember they're both nearly a hundred years old. They only look like kids. And act like kids most of the time. Especially Salix.

I sigh and dig a soy milk out of my backpack. As I drink, Rosa trots over to a frozen puddle. She coughs out a ball of blue flame. The puddle melts. Then she laps up the water.

"Nice," Salix says.

So that answers that question. I guess Rosa *is* still magical.

Salix tells me he and Finola will keep watch so I can rest. I feel like I'm too nervous, but as soon as I close my eyes, Rosa curls up in my lap. Then I relax a bit and drift off.

What seems like only a few seconds later, someone is shaking me.

"Blue! Blue!" Finola whispers urgently. "Wake up!"

I snap awake.

"It's midnight," Finola says. "The witches are here."

I peer into the darkness. The cemetery is across the churchyard, behind a high wrought-iron fence. I can just make out several dark figures picking their way through the tombstones.

"Where are Salix and Rosa?" I ask.

Finola frowns. "They're looking for a way past the fence," she says.

I look back at the cemetery. "Can't we just open the gate?" I ask. "Isn't that how the witches got in?"

"You can," Finola says. "But those witches are human. The fence is iron. Faeries can't get past iron. It hurts us."

"Iron hurts you too? Like silver?" I know there are quite a few ways to deter Faeries. I guess iron is another of them.

"It's worse than silver in a way," Finola says. "It makes us feel very heavy. So heavy we can't breathe. Then we can die."

At that moment Salix and Rosa come running back.

"There's no way through," Salix says.

"Even Rosa can't get through?"

"No," Salix says. "She's definitely a Faerie dog now. I don't know how that happened. I didn't think it was possible. I wonder what powers she has."

"We'll worry about that later," Finola says. She turns to me. "What do you want to do, Blue?"

"I have no choice," I say. "I'll have to confront the witches alone."

⇾ ★ ⇽

My heart pounds as I tiptoe down to the gate. It's not locked, thank goodness. I push it, and it creaks a tiny bit. I open it just enough to squeeze through. Looking behind me, I can see Salix and Finola watching. Rosa is pulling on her leash, but she's not barking. I think she knows she needs to be quiet.

I step lightly, hiding behind tombstones, until I'm close enough to the witches to see what they're doing. They're standing in a circle, holding hands. A dozen candles burn in the center of the circle. The witches begin to chant.

My heart was pounding before, but now I think it might stop. What are they doing? Are they going to raise zombies? Some sort of demon?

I duck across to the next tombstone. Now that I'm closer, I can hear them.

"Parking restrictions on Queen Street from three to six on weekdays," they chant.

Parking restrictions? That seems kind of… ordinary for witches.

"Fines for using gas-powered lawn mowers on weekend mornings," the chant continues.

Is this a witches' coven or a city council meeting?

"Season tickets for the Blue Jays…"

So I guess they like baseball. I'm starting to wonder if I'm in the right graveyard.

Suddenly the chanting stops. "Who's there?" one of the witches shouts. She turns and looks right at me. "Come forward, child," she says kindly. "Do you have a request for the sisters of night? Funding for a new school bus? A potion for acne?"

These witches are nothing like I expected them to be. I step out from behind the tombstone. I get closer to the circle of candles. One of the witches beckons me with a curved hand.

They are all dressed in long black coats. Their boots are black too. Some of them have their hoods up. Some are wearing loose black hats. The one who beckoned me steps into the candlelight. I can see that she's very old. Her white hair hangs in two braids.

"Good evening, young man," she says. "I am Mrs. Brooks. What do the stars call you?"

"The stars?" I ask. "I doubt the stars even know I exist. My name is Blue. I'm looking for my mother."

Mrs. Brooks turns. "Is the mother of Blue in the circle?" she asks. All the other witches shake their heads.

"She's not a—one of you," I clarify. "I was told you might be able to help me find her. I think she's with someone you know. Someone called Barbara?"

Mrs. Brooks reacts. She takes a tiny step back. The other witches seem to shiver, as though a breeze has passed over them.

"Come closer, Blue who is unknown by the stars," Mrs. Brooks says.

Faintly I hear Rosa give a sharp bark. I know it's a warning. But what can I do? I have to find my mother. I need their help. It's past midnight now. Dawn is only hours away. If I don't find Mom by then...

"Come, Blue," Mrs. Brooks says. "I have something for you." She holds out a marble. Kevin said witches often give these as gifts. It seems rude not to take it.

I hold out my hand, and Mrs. Brooks drops it in my palm. I slip it into my pocket.

"It will help you see the stars," she says.

"What stars?"

"The ones that don't know you exist, I suppose," she says. "Come closer, Blue. We don't bite."

I step forward. Just as I reach Mrs. Brooks, she throws something down at the base of a gravestone. I see what it is. Another marble. The candlelight glints on it for a second.

Then Mrs. Brooks smashes it with her boot.

Vile green smoke pours out. I try to hold my breath, but it doesn't help. I can hear Rosa barking frantically. Salix and Finola yell, but they sound far away. My body starts to sag. My knees give out. I fall, hitting the gravestone with a crack. The candles blur in my vision. I fumble for the hilt of my ghost sword, but my fingers won't work.

Just as I feel myself slipping into darkness, I see someone. Another witch in a dark robe enters the circle. It's her. The bog witch. Barbara. She peers down at me.

Then everything goes black.

Chapter Eight

I wake up with my face in something foul-smelling. Jerking back, I realize what it is. A mop! A gross, old, damp mop. Dragging my sleeve over my face, I sit up. I'm in a narrow room. The only light is from a red emergency sign. As my eyes adjust, I see where I am. It's a kind of utility closet. The large kind you might find in a store or a school. There are racks of brooms and shelves full of cleaning stuff.

I appear to be alone.

"Salix? Finola?" I whisper.

"Blue?" a voice says. I jerk back as someone jumps out from behind a cabinet.

"Mom!"

I nearly trip over a bucket as I run into her arms. She hugs me tightly.

"Blue, oh baby boy," she says, squeezing me. "What are you doing here?"

"Where are we?" I ask.

"No idea," she says. "I just woke up. I think I've been enchanted."

I strain my eyes, looking around at the shelves. At last I find a flashlight. I flick it on and point it at the ceiling. Finally Mom and I can see each other properly. She holds my face and kisses my forehead until I squirm away.

"How did you get here?" I ask. "Do you remember?"

"No," she says. "The last thing I remember is sweeping the kitchen. Then…flying. Then just a glimpse of the Crosswood. And then I woke up here a few minutes ago."

We sit down on some boxes of hand towels.

"We're in Toronto," I say. "Oren helped me get here." I update her on everything else that has happened. Olea. The witches in the graveyard. Barbara.

"A bog witch," Mom says. "Is that bad?"

"She turned one of my friends into a swan."

Mom puts her hand over her mouth for a second.

"I wish I had never made that deal with Olea," she says. "None of this would have happened."

"I'd be dead if you hadn't," I remind her.

She nods sadly. "What do you think Olea wants with us?" she asks.

I decide against telling her everything Oren and I discussed. She doesn't need to know that Olea might have some spell involving me in mind. Some spell that needs a firstborn son. If Mom knew that, she would just try to sacrifice herself again.

She would do anything for me. Even die. That thought makes my eyes fill with tears. I look away for a few seconds.

"Blue?" Mom says softly. "Are you okay?"

I blink away the tears. "I'm fine," I say. "I'm just thinking. First we should get out of this closet."

"The door is locked," Mom says. "I tried it just before I realized you were here."

I stand up and inspect the door. Yep. It's locked. But there is a small window above it. I pull a box over and stand on it. Then I look through the window.

I see mostly darkness but also...*stars*. I think I see stars. That makes me remember the marbles in my pocket. One of them, from the witch in the graveyard, is supposed to help me see stars. Could she have been trying to help me even while she helped Barbara, the bog witch, capture me? It seemed like the witches in the graveyard might be scared of Barbara. Maybe...

I try the door handle again. Pull on it. Shake it. The door is locked tight.

Pulling both marbles out of my pocket, I take a proper look at the one Mrs. Brooks gave me. It's all metal instead of glass like the other one. Metal. Like a key? It seems it might be more useful than the other one—the friend or fiend finder. The last thing we need here in the closet is a fiend.

Once again I don't have much choice. I have to try it. I drop the marble on the floor and stamp on it hard.

"Blue!" Mom cries. "What are you doing?"

A fine silvery smoke wafts out from the crushed marble. It floats up in a wisp and curls into the door lock.

The lock clicks, and I open the door.

⇒ ★ ⇐

I hold Mom back while I peek out the door. We are in some kind of large, dimly lit round room. The outer walls are floor-to-ceiling windows. Outside the windows I see only stars.

Are we in a spaceship? That would be an unexpected twist.

"Hello?" I say. I don't get a reply. Wherever we are, we seem to be alone.

"There's no one here," I tell Mom. She follows me out into the round room.

"Oh, wow," Mom says. "I think I know where we are." She moves toward the windows. I follow her.

Stars. A full moon giving off blue light. And below that, through thin mist, a city. The nighttime streets spread out to the horizon. I didn't know cities could be so huge. Now I'm worried we might be on another planet.

"We're in the CN Tower," Mom says.

"*The* CN Tower?" I say. "So we're still in Toronto?"

We walk around the whole circle. On one side the city disappears, replaced by a swath of darkness.

"That's Lake Ontario," Mom says.

We return to the city-view side. The mist below us seems to thicken, making the lights on the streets and buildings fade.

Wait.

"Are those *clouds*?" I ask. "Are we above the clouds?"

Mom presses her face against the glass. "It looks like it," she says. "I think we might be on the upper observation deck too. More than a thousand feet up."

I take a step back from the glass. "Let's get out of here."

We try the elevator first, but when we press the button, nothing happens. No lights go on, no hum of the elevator approaching.

"It's probably deactivated for the night," Mom says. "What time is it anyway?"

I check my watch. "Oh no," I gasp.

"What is it?"

"It's nearly seven a.m.," I say. "We must have been unconscious for hours."

"Well, at least the sun will come up soon," Mom says. "And the tower will open. They'll turn on the elevator. We can get out."

"Yeah, but…" I think carefully about how much to say. "The message Oren gave me was that I had to get you before dawn on the solstice. Or… you know…"

"I die," Mom says. She thinks for a moment. "Maybe the witch has some kind of spell that needs…my liver or something."

I know she's only half kidding. "Something like that," I say.

"Let's take the stairs," Mom says. She leads us around the circle again. Following some safety posters, we find a door marked *Emergency Exit. Alarm Will Sound*. I figure setting off an alarm could only help us. I pull on the door handle.

Nothing happens. The door doesn't open. The alarm doesn't sound.

"It's locked?" Mom says. "Emergency doors aren't supposed to be locked."

"It must be enchanted," I say. "They want to keep us here." I kick the door, frustrated. "Do you have your phone? We could call the police."

Mom shakes her head. "I don't have my phone. I think they must have taken it from me."

"If only I had my *own* phone," I say under my breath.

"What?" Mom asks in a small voice.

"If only I had my *own phone*, Mom!" I feel myself getting angry. I know I shouldn't be angry with Mom, but she's the only one here right now. "It's normal for teenagers to have phones. And laptops. And the internet. Why do we have to live like cavemen?"

Mom looks shocked. She crosses her arms. "I'm just trying to keep you all safe."

"Safe?" I say. Now I'm really venting. I'm saying things I've wanted to say for months. Years maybe. "If you'd lived in a normal house with a phone when I got sick, when I was little, you could have just called an ambulance! You never would have met Olea! None of this would have happened!"

"Blue!" Mom says. To my horror, her eyes fill with tears. "I didn't have a choice. The cottage was all I had. I had nowhere else to go!"

"You could have gotten a phone!"

"I had no money!" Mom yells. "Your father had left us. I was all alone."

Suddenly my anger is gone. Suddenly I'm thinking about our little cottage in a different light. I'd always thought the way we lived was Mom's choice. And I'd thought her accepting help from Olea was a choice too. And her taking on the twins. But for the first time I realize she might not have had a choice. She was poor and alone. And she was scared.

I reach for her, but she pulls away. And before I can say something to make it all better, the air around us begins to shimmer. The smell of strawberries wafts up from under the emergency door. Mom and I step back as the door opens.

Olea is standing there.

Chapter Nine

"Blue Jasper," Olea says in a teasing tone. "You should speak to your mother with more respect. I heard your yelling from three stories down."

"Don't speak to my son!" Mom says. She wraps her arms around me protectively.

Olea is flanked by the same two Faerie guards she had in Witherwood. I really wish I'd killed them with my ghost sword when I had the chance.

My ghost sword! I reach for it at my waist, but it's not there. The witches must have taken it from me.

"Looking for this, Blue?" Olea says. She waves her hand around. One of the safety posters on the wall splits in half and drifts down to the floor. "A ghost sword is a rare treasure."

"That's mine," I say.

"Finders keepers," Olea says. She tucks the sword away. "Take the woman," she says. One of her guards dashes forward and grabs Mom before I can stop him. He bounds across the floor and dives right at the windows.

"No!" I say.

One of the windows shatters, leaving a gaping hole at the edge of the observation deck. The guard sails out into the dark with Mom. Through the mist and cloud I can just see his large, green, batlike wings unfurl. They catch the wind and he swoops upwards, disappearing into the sky. Mom's screams fade in the distance.

"Goodbye, Blue," Olea says. The other guard grabs her and leaps for the window too. His wings are bright yellow and feathered, like a cockatoo's. I watch them fly away until they are just a speck in the dark.

Cold wind blows in through the broken window. I slink back to the broom closet. Finding a mop with a metal handle, I unscrew the mop part. Now I have a metal staff. At least that's some defense against my sword if Olea comes back.

Of course she's going to come back. It's me she wants.

I go back out to the observation deck, avoiding the broken window. I press my face against the window facing the city. I can't believe there are millions of people down there. Including all kinds of police officers and firefighters. There are rescue boats on the lake. Even soldiers probably. There's probably an army base.

But none of them can help me.

I feel more alone than I ever have. And I miss my friends.

My friends! I wonder where they are. That makes me remember the other marble in my pocket.

Friend finder.

Or *fiend* finder. It must be friend finder. Kevin at the store said that witches give them as little gifts. Why would anyone, even a witch, give someone a spell to summon *fiends*? It must be friend. Right?

Part of me doesn't care. I'm not even sure what a fiend is, but anything would be better than being stuck up here alone. And maybe a fiend would defend me. It might get magically attached to me and owe me wishes. Like a genie or something.

Or...it might eat me.

Or I might be overthinking this. Maybe it's just an ordinary marble.

But there's only one way to find out.

I step back from the window and drop the marble on the floor, then smash it with my boot.

The deck fills with bright light as if something has exploded. I fall back against the inner wall, shielding my eyes from the glare.

When my vision clears, Salix, Finola and Rosa are standing there.

They look very surprised.

$$\Rightarrow \star \Leftarrow$$

Rosa barks and starts jumping all over me.

"Blue!" Salix says, rushing forward. "Thank frogs! We've been searching for you for hours!"

"How did we get here?" Finola asks.

"Remember the witch in the Wherewood? The one who gave us the potion so I could breathe underwater? She also gave me a magic marble. Like those ones in the store."

"A friend finder?" Finola says. "Good thing you've been carrying it around all this time."

I don't answer. But I make a mental note to thank Indigo for putting it in my pocket.

Rosa is still jumping on me and tugging on her leash. Salix struggles to keep her controlled.

"Rosa, settle down!" I say. "Settle!"

Salix ends up tying her leash to the closet-door handle. Her leash is long enough that she can move around. But not so long that she could fall out of the broken window.

Salix, Finola and I sit in a circle nearby and discuss what to do.

"What do you think Olea's plan is?" Salix asks.

"Oren thinks she's trying to get her magic back," I say.

"But how?" Finola asks.

"I'm not sure," I say, hesitating before I go on. "But Oren thought she might use a spell that needs a firstborn son. A *human* firstborn son."

"Oh no," Finola says with a gasp.

"Do you know what spell it is?" I ask.

"No," she says. "But it must be very wicked. Witchcraft that uses parts of humans is very cursed and dark magic."

"*Parts* of humans?!" I cry.

"That really doesn't sound good," Salix says unhelpfully.

"You think?" I reply. I'm beginning to think I might just jump out the window and take my chances with the clouds.

"Okay, don't panic," Finola says. "When…er…if they come back, our priority is getting that witch away from Olea. Without her, Olea won't be able to do the spell."

"How will we do that?" I ask. "Olea has those

guards with her. And I don't even have my sword."

"Let me worry about the witch," Finola says darkly. "I've been waiting a long time to pay her back for what she did to me."

Salix squeezes her hand.

"Without the witch, Olea's plans are pond scum," Salix says. "Right?"

I think about that for a few seconds. When you're dealing with Faeries, you have to think things through carefully. There are all kinds of tricks and surprises they can come up with.

"If Finola and the witch are out of the picture, that leaves Olea, Mom, me and Salix," I say.

"And Rosa," Salix says. "And maybe two guards." He makes a face. "I don't like our chances."

I think so hard my brain starts to hurt. What else could Olea do? She's smart. She'll have a backup plan. Then I realize something.

"Why do you think those guards are still with her?" I ask. "Even after everything she's done?"

Salix and Finola both shrug.

"She's human now," I say. "She can command them. I bet she used their full names and commanded them to do all this stuff." I start counting things off on my fingers. "To kidnap Mom. To send a message to Oren. To find and bribe a witch. To fly us up here. To snatch Mom again..."

"She can only use three commands on each of them," Finola says. "It seems like she might have used up all the commands."

We fall silent for a few seconds.

"But she could command *me*," Salix says quietly.

"Does she know your full name?" Finola asks, her eyes wide.

"No," Salix says.

I clutch him by the shoulder. "Salix," I say gravely. "If you're my friend, if you're my *best* friend, you must not, ever, under any circumstances, tell me or Mom or Olea or *any* human your full name."

"I *am* your best friend," Salix says. He takes my other shoulder and gives it a squeeze.

"Do you promise?" I ask.

Salix meets my eyes, nodding. "A Faerie promise can't be broken," he says. "I promise."

Before we can say more, Rosa starts barking. Outside the broken window I see two shapes approaching in the dark sky.

It's the Faerie guards. One of them has Mom. The other one has Olea—and the witch.

Chapter Ten

The guards land just inside the window and set Mom, Olea and the witch down. Both guards are panting. They shake their wings and retract them before stepping to the side to stand guard.

"Hello, Barbara," Finola says coldly as she shrugs off her coat and unfurls her wings. "Remember me?"

Barbara barely has time to shake the snow from her hair. Finola leaps across the deck and snatches her. They both go sailing out the window.

"What are you standing there for?" Olea shrieks at her guards. "Go after them."

Maybe I'm imagining it, but the guards don't seem very enthusiastic about flying out into the cold again. They stumble to the window and leap out. Salix runs to the deck's edge and leans out, trying to see Finola as she sails away through the sky.

One of the guards catches up with her. He grabs hold of one of her wings, sending all of them twirling down toward the clouds.

"NO!" Salix yells.

For a second I think he is going to leap after them, but instead he pushes one hand forward. A jet of water shoots out! This must be one of his new magical skills. The guard holding Finola's wing is soaked. He lets go and tries to fly off. But his waterlogged wings start to freeze. He loses altitude rapidly. Then he falls, whooshing deeper into the clouds and disappearing.

Before the second guard can catch up to Finola, Salix shoots a jet of water at him too. It soaks and freezes one of his wings, sending him wildly off course. Finola sails upward, the cold wind catching her. Seconds later she's too far away to see. The second guard flails around just above the clouds before finally sinking into them.

I turn back to Olea, who is pale with shock and fury. Mom twists away from her. She scrambles toward me.

"Blue! She has a—"

But Olea cuts her off. "Silence!"

Salix and I spread out, moving away from the window, and try to close in Olea on either side.

Olea raises her arms. One hand looks empty, but I know she's holding the ghost sword. In her other hand she holds a small knife, barely bigger than a butter knife. It doesn't even look very sharp. I don't know what she thinks she is going to do with that. She backs away from us.

"Not so brave without your witch now, are you?" I say. "Or your guards. You're only human. And it's three against one." Behind Olea, Rosa barks. "Four if you include Rosa."

Olea edges toward Mom, who is crawling back to the wall by the elevator. Is she injured? I hold my mop handle like an ax and move to block Olea from getting to her.

Rosa barks urgently and tugs on her leash, rattling the closet door. I'm tempted to let her go. She has protected me before. But she might not know that we're a hundred stories up. What if she jumps out the window opening?

Salix approaches Olea from her other side as she sneers at me. "I don't need a witch," she says. "I don't need guards. I have something better." She flicks the knife in her hand. With a shriek, she whirls on Salix, leaping on him. They both fall back and roll dangerously close to the opening.

Salix drops his glamour. The cold wind buffets his green hair. His face contorts with pain. Olea has her knife pressed against his face.

"Silver!" he cries. "The knife is silver!"

⇒ ★ ⇐

Silver! Silver kills Faeries. It burns them.

Salix moans with pain and tries to pull himself away from Olea. She has him pinned next to her, with the empty space beyond the broken glass behind them.

"Salix Flapfoot," Olea says with a snarl. "Tell me your full name!"

I take a step forward, wielding my pathetic mop handle.

"No closer!" Olea says. "The tiniest cut will kill your friend."

I stop. I don't actually know how silver works on Faeries. "Is that true?" I ask. If Olea were still a Faerie, she wouldn't be able to lie. But she's a human now. And we lie all the time. "Salix, is that true?"

He manages a small nod. Olea adjusts the position of the knife. I can see she has the blunt side pressed to Salix's cheek. I can also see the silver is burning him, leaving red welts on his greenish skin.

"Let him go!" I yell. But I don't move. I'm frozen to the spot.

"Now, Salix Flapfoot," Olea says through gritted teeth. "Your full name."

"Even if he does give it to you, I won't command him," I say. "It won't work."

"Nor will I," Mom says. I risk a glance at her. She's curled up against the wall. Rosa has stretched out her leash as far as she can and stands protectively in front of Mom.

Olea just laughs. "I don't *need* either of you to command him. You made me human, remember, Blue? Now I have that human power. Now I can command Faeries with their full names."

She's right. This has been her plan B all along. If Salix tells her his full name, she can command him to give up his power. His magic will flow out of him and into her. It will make her magical again. Probably. It makes me wonder what her plan A was. Something to do with my blood or organs? Some horrible spell? Was she trying to become *more* powerful than a Faerie?

Then I realize something. When you command a Faerie to give up their power, it just pours out of them. It becomes wild magic, which flows into anything or anyone nearby that is non-magical.

That happened to me once. It made me magical for a few minutes before it ran out. But it's dangerous. I barely survived. If it flows into Mom, it could hurt her or even kill her.

If Salix's magic flowed into Olea, she would stay magical, because she has Faerie blood. That's how it works. But it could flow into any of us. And Olea knows that. Which means if she gets Salix's name and tries to command him, we can't be here. Me. Mom. Rosa, too.

So if Salix gives up his name, Olea probably plans to kill us all.

Salix moans with pain. His green eyes roll back.

"Your name, Salix Flapfoot," Olea says. "Your whole name. The one known only to you."

He won't do it. He can't. He made a Faerie promise.

Olea releases him suddenly. He slumps back and drags himself a few feet away from the window.

"Fine," Olea says. "If pain won't convince you, perhaps this will."

She moves so quickly, it's hard to believe she no longer has magic. Before I can react, she leaps at me, swinging the ghost sword. I barely dodge it. I stumble back, falling on my butt. The mop handle goes flying. Then Olea is on me, pressing the ghost sword against my throat. And she's not using the blunt side.

"Your full name, Salix Flapfoot," Olea says. "Or your friend dies."

By this time Salix has pulled himself to his feet. He stares at me for a moment. The swirling dark sky behind him frames his green face.

"Don't do it, Salix," I say. "She'll take your magic. She'll kill us anyway."

He nods and gives me a little smile.

Then he turns, and jumping through the window opening, he tumbles into the dark.

Chapter Eleven

"Salix! No!" I scream.

Olea drags me to the window opening. I just catch a glimpse of Salix falling. He seems to shimmer as the clouds envelop him. Then he's gone.

"SALIX!!!"

There's no answer but the cold wind.

He's gone. Gone. My best friend just gave up his life for mine.

The rage that bubbles up inside me feels like magic. Like I could defeat a thousand wicked Faeries. I twist out of Olea's grasp and kick her in the side. She barely avoids falling out the window. That gives me time to scramble away. I grab the mop handle, spinning as Olea stalks after me.

That's when I realize Olea must have a plan C too. Her plan C is to kill me just for the fun of it. Mom too, probably.

"Mom, get out of here!" I say. "Take the stairs! Take Rosa and run!"

Rosa barks, straining on her leash.

"I'm not leaving you!" Mom yells. She ducks into the broom closet instead and comes out with the metal nozzle of a vacuum cleaner.

"I grew up sword fighting," Olea says snidely. "I trained in it, as all Faerie queens do. What battle training do *you* have?"

Mom's face hardens. "I'm the mother of *twins*," she says. Wielding the vacuum nozzle like an ax, she moves toward Olea's other side. Now Olea is hemmed in. Me and Mom on two sides, and the dark cavern of night behind her. Olea has the silver knife in one hand and the ghost sword in the other. She waves them around gracefully.

Mom and I both stiffen as Olea steps forward.

"Humans can't defeat Faeries," Olea says. "We're far too powerful. Give up."

"You're not a Faerie anymore," I say. "You're human. There's no Faerie magic here. It's just us."

"A boy," Olea sneers. "And a woman who bakes muffins."

Mom gasps. "I'm a qualified medical receptionist!"

Olea pauses for a moment. "I have no idea what that means," she says. "Nor do I care."

She leaps at me, bringing the ghost sword down. It's hard for me to block something I can't see. But I manage it somehow. The sword clangs against my mop handle. When I roll away, I see the sword has left a deep welt in the metal. I don't think I can deflect many more hits like that.

Olea whirls on Mom, slashing with the sword. But Mom twists away. She spins and slams the vacuum nozzle down on Olea's other wrist. The tiny silver knife goes pinging across the floor. Mom leaps for it, snatching it up.

Olea mocks her. "How is that little knife going to help you?" she asks.

Mom presses against the wall and edges back toward the stairwell. I hope she's planning on taking Rosa and getting out of here.

Olea advances on me again, bringing her sword down. *CLANG!* It bounces off my mop handle, leaving it bent.

CLANG! I swipe away another strike. But I lose my balance and tumble backward. Winded, I roll away, slashing with the bent mop handle. Olea hacks at me. Finally the mop handle gives.

It splits in two, leaving me with a jagged stump.

Suddenly I feel Mom grab the hood of my coat. She yanks me, and I go sliding across the floor. I land in a heap next to Rosa. She barks frantically. All I can do is watch in horror as Olea advances on Mom. Mom kicks out and somehow manages to knock Olea off her feet. I roll over and start getting up. Mom shouts at me.

"Blue!" she yells, tossing something. The little knife. She's giving me her last weapon. Our last chance, small as it is. I blink at it once. Then I dive for Rosa. No time to undo knots. I slice right through her leash.

"Mrs. Rosa Guzman! I command you!" I scream. "Attack Olea Briar!"

⇉ ★ ⇇

Rosa snarls and seems to inflate. Her fur stands on end. Baring her teeth, she bounds across the deck. Olea clambers to her feet, swinging the ghost sword. Rosa dodges it as though she can see it. Maybe she can. Maybe Faerie dogs have special senses. Like how regular dogs have excellent hearing and smell. Olea slashes wildly, but Rosa ducks and swerves.

Olea edges back toward the opening to the dark. Wind blows a gust of freezing air around us. So cold my breath catches. I start to tremble.

Olea entices Rosa to follow her. I know what she's doing. Olea is trying to get Rosa close enough to the edge to push her off. I try to get up, but there's something wrong with my knee. I think I twisted it. I yelp with pain. Mom takes a swing at Olea from behind her back. Olea blocks it. This gives Rosa a chance to bite Olea on the ankle. Olea screams.

"Filthy beast!" she says. She flicks out her leg, and Rosa lets go. She slides dangerously close to the fatal gap in the windows. Her claws scrape on the smooth floor. At the last second she stops herself, turning on Olea with a vicious growl.

Maybe I'm seeing things. It seems like Rosa's eyes are glowing red. Olea slashes at her. This time the sword nips one of Rosa's ears. She yelps, but the hit just makes her angrier. She jumps up and clamps her teeth into Olea's wrist. Olea won't let go of the sword. Her hand is clenched so tight, I can see her knuckles turning white. Rosa hangs from her, scratching at Olea's face with her paws. Olea stumbles backward a step. Then another.

"No!" I cry. Ignoring the pain in my knee, I stagger after them. Just as they reach the window opening, I dive. With a screech, Olea loses her footing. I lunge for them, just getting my fingers around her free wrist. The momentum of her fall drags me forward until I'm hanging over the edge. One of my hands is around Olea's wrist. The other hand flails, trying to find a handhold. Below us, Rosa still clings to Olea's other wrist, swinging in the icy wind.

Just as I think I'm about to slip out and to certain death, I feel Mom grab me by the ankles.

Olea's face breaks into an evil grin. That's when I realize that at some point she switched the ghost sword to her other hand. The hand attached to the wrist I'm now holding. And I think maybe Olea has a plan D—to cut my arm off. She twists her wrist with a cruel grimace. I feel the edge of the sword slice my elbow. I scream with pain. My arm spasms.

And I let go.

Chapter Twelve

"Blue!" I hear Mom yell, but I can't see anything except Olea and Rosa plummeting down. Olea screams, and as she loses her grip on the ghost sword, I catch a glimpse of it, reflecting in the moonlight. Rosa lets go of her wrist, and they spin away from each other.

"Rosa!" I scream. "NO! ROSA!"

Then, as they both tumble and disappear in the clouds, I shout as loudly as I can, with every breath I have left.

"MRS. ROSA GUZMAN! I COMMAND YOU! FLY!"

Mom yanks me back onto the deck, pulling me into her arms.

My whole body feels like jelly.

"Rosa!" I wail. I know I've only had her for a few months, but it feels like forever. And now she's gone. Fallen to her death. Along with Olea, who is only human after all.

Olea's dead. She's finally dead.

But Mom's not dead. And I'm not dead.

I only *feel* dead.

Rosa is gone. Salix is gone. And Finola will probably never speak to me again. Mom holds me tight. She clamps her hand over the gash on my elbow. It hurts so much that I press my face into her coat sleeve so she won't see me cry.

My tears freeze on my face.

Then, over the wind whooshing through the broken window, I hear something. A faint yelp.

No. Not a yelp.

A *bark*.

"Rosa?"

I untangle myself from Mom, and we both crawl toward the window. I hear the noise again. This time not so much a bark as a roar. I strain my eyes, trying to see down into the dark clouds. Suddenly a dark shape bursts out in a puff of mist.

"Rosa!"

She…she grew wings! As she gets closer, I realize she grew more than wings. She grew in size. Nearly doubled in size. And she grew a long tail like…

Well. Like a dragon. She looks like a dog crossed with a dragon.

"Oh my goodness," Mom says.

Rosa flaps her large leathery wings gracefully as she rises.

We move back as Rosa reaches the opening. Folding her wings, she glides in. She slides a bit clumsily as she lands. I suppose that's to be expected. She did just learn how to fly.

My command, maybe my last one to Rosa ever, worked. She flew!

I have a flying dog!

Rosa drips icy water on the floor. She shakes herself, spraying me and Mom.

"Rosa! Stop!" I say. But she keeps shaking. And as she does, she transforms back into a dog. She's still a little bigger than she was. And there's a hint of dragon in her face. But she looks like a dog again. She stops shaking and sits.

I fall down on my knees and throw my arms around her. Dog or dragon, she's alive.

"Blue," Mom says after a moment. "We should get out of here. Look."

I turn and look. Through the windows to the east, the sunrise is just visible on the distant horizon.

We head down the stairs. Mom helps me. I rest one hand on Rosa's head for support. But a few flights down my knee is so painful I'm seeing stars. Mom has wrapped my scarf around my bleeding elbow. The last thing we need to do is leave a trail of blood on the stairs of the CN Tower.

Just when I'm sure I'm about to pass out, we hear someone coming up the other way. Mom looks at me, stricken. There's nowhere to hide! But seconds later a red cloak swishes into view on the landing below us.

It's Oren!

He bounds up the last flight of stairs. I collapse in a pile at his feet.

"Finola sent me," he says, kneeling next to me. He waves magical healing over my knee and elbow. "I arrived just as—" He stops, frowning.

"Just as what?" Mom asks.

"Just as Olea fell," he says with a grim expression. "She's dead."

"Faerie dead or human dead?" I ask. I don't know if there's a difference. It seems as though there should be.

"Dead dead," Oren says. "I promise, she won't bother you again."

My body goes cold, and I start to shiver. As we try to continue down the stairs, I stumble. Oren catches me and lifts me up.

"He's exhausted," Mom says. "And probably in shock."

Oren looks down on my face with a little smile.

"Sleep now," he says.

First I see sparkles again. Then everything goes black.

⇒ ★ ⇐

I wake up in my own bed, facing the wall, Rosa curled up beside me.

"At last you're awake," someone says.

I roll over.

"Salix!"

Salix is sitting at my desk chair. He's sharpening a pencil. On the floor below him is a giant pile of pencil shavings. It looks like he has sharpened every pencil in the house.

"I like this toy," he says, showing me the pencil sharpener.

"It's not—never mind," I say. "You can keep it. I have another one somewhere."

Salix grins and puts the sharpener in his pocket.

"Why aren't you dead?" I ask.

"Don't sound so disappointed," Salix says. "I turned myself into water when I fell. It was the only thing I could think of to do. As I passed through the clouds, something weird happened. I kind of froze into a million little pieces."

"A million pieces?" I think about that for a second. "Snow! You turned into snow!"

Salix nods a little shyly. "I guess I did. I floated down and landed safely. Well, in a million little pieces, but safely. Finally I started to melt back into water. Then I turned back into me. By that time, Oren was just coming down the stairs with you."

"And he brought us back here?"

"Yes," Salix says. "But he had to go back to Toronto. To…deal with…" His voice trails off.

"With Olea?" I say. "So the humans don't make a fuss like they always do?"

Salix smiles. "*You're* a human, Blue," he says. "Oren sent a message back with a Will-o'-the-Wisp. As far as the humans think, the windstorm blew out a panel of glass in that tower place. No one was injured."

"What did Oren do with Olea? With her body?" I ask.

"He took it back to Faerieland," Salix answers. "To Witherwood actually. He buried her there."

I think about that for a moment. I hope there's no zombie-style, dead-raising magic in Witherwood. But Oren promised that Olea won't bother me again. He couldn't make that promise if he didn't think it was true. Maybe Olea really is gone forever.

"What about the bog witch?" I ask. "And Finola? Is she okay?"

"Finola is fine. The bog witch has been imprisoned in Fenwood. She has five years to think about what she's done. And Oren made her promise never to use magic or witchcraft again. And you know what that means."

"Yes," I say. "Faerie promises can't be broken. By Faerie or by human. And the twins are okay? And Mom?"

Salix pats me. "Everyone is fine," he says. He looks older than I remember. Maybe turning into snow and back into a person has made him grow up a little.

But then, I think, I probably look older too. And not just from growing up.

"You look pale, Blue," Salix says. "I'll bring you something to eat. I think your mom is making soup. With tomatoes and rice! Can you imagine?" He shakes his head as he goes out into the kitchen.

Mom's tomato rice soup is one of my favorites. Now that Salix has mentioned it, I can smell it. My mouth waters. I fall back on my pillow.

I *feel* pale. And I'm *starving*. I have no idea how long I was asleep. And I can't remember the last time I ate something.

But I also can't remember the last time I felt so relaxed. Olea can't hurt us anymore. She can't hurt anyone. Part of me is sad that she died—she was the twins' birth mother, after all—but most of me is just happy that Mom and Indigo and Violet are safe now. Salix and Finola are safe. Oren is safe. Rosa is safe.

The Faerie Woods, and our wood, are safe at last.

Knowing how Faeries work, and magic, it probably won't stay that way forever. But for now, I'm going to eat my soup. I'm going to take a bath. Maybe I'll read a book.

And I'm going to ask Mom if I can have a phone or a laptop.

Again.

Blue returns to the Faerie woods where an old enemy is waiting.

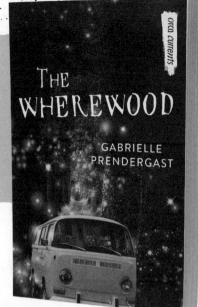

Magic and the human realm just don't mix.

orca currents

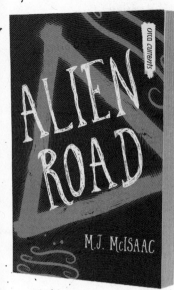

ALIEN ROAD

M.J. McISAAC

orca currents

A BOAT TRIP THROUGH THE LEGENDARY BERMUDA TRIANGLE

JENNIFER HAS A BIG SECRET—SHE CAN MOVE OBJECTS WITH HER MIND.

WILLPOWER

MARTY CHAN

orca currents

Gabrielle Prendergast has written many books for young people, including the BC Book Prize-winning *Zero Repeat Forever*, the Westchester Award winner *Audacious*, and the first two instalments in the Faerie Woods series in the Orca Currents line, *The Crosswood* and *The Wherewood*. She lives in Vancouver, British Columbia, with her family.

For more information on all the books

in the Orca Currents line, please visit

orcabook.com